CRITTER CAKES
&FROG TEA

Tales and treats from the Emerald River

by Marie Rudisill

Crane Hill Publishers
Birmingham, Alabama

Copyright 1994 by Marie Rudisill

Published by Crane Hill Publishers
First edition, first printing

Library of Congress Cataloging-in-Publication Data

Rudisill, Marie.
    Critter Cakes & Frog Tea : Tales and Treats from the Emerald River
    / by Marie Rudisill : illustrations by Robin McLendon.
        p.   cm.
    ISBN 1-881548-09-0 : $12. 95
    1. Cookery—Juvenile literature. [1. Cookery]   I. McLendon,
    Robin, 1960-   ill.   II. Title III. Title: Critter Cakes and Frog
    Tea.
TX652.5.R83   1994
641.5'123—dc20   94-9086
                                                         CIP
                                                          AC

Design and production by *icon graphics*, Birmingham, Alabama

Crane Hill Publishers
2923 Crescent Avenue
Birmingham, Alabama 35209

Dedicated to a small boy whose dreams of snowflakes
and sunsets came true . . .
Truman Capote

From his Aunt Marie

Contents

Critter Cakes & Frog Tea

Tales and Treats from the Emerald River

WELCOME TO EMERALD RIVER

In a warm place far away from here, there is a great old house that looks out over Emerald River. It has been washed to a gray silvery color by many years of wind and rain, and its shingles are velvety green with moss. From its long upper porch you can look out over the water.

Along the banks of the river, the grass under the trees is purpled with wood-violets that have heart-shaped leaves as big as a puppy's ears.

The ditches and canals that crisscross the fields this way and that make a great checkerboard of the land around the river. The squares of this great checkerboard turn different colors with each change of season. In the fall there are squares of white cotton and squares of yellow corn. In the spring the squares of black plowed land and squares of bright-green sprouting crops show off the richness that the Emerald River leaves with us as it meanders on its way to the sea. It is truly a grand place to live.

RED RIP THE PIG

Besides being the residence of a farm family, this is also the residence of a rather select group of animals, if I do say so myself. I, of course, am the leader of this group of animals. Please allow me to introduce myself—I am Red-Rip the Pig, and it is my job to oversee the planting of the garden and also the harvesting.

After the garden is planted, it is a chore to keep the other animals out of it. I have to keep the twin raccoons out of the corn, the ducks from picking the young string beans, the rat from eating the strawberries, the cats from puncturing the vegetables with their claws, and I have the most awful time keeping Mr. Frog from picking the beautiful orange blossoms off of the squash. He vows that he must have them for his afternoon teas.

All this is my responsibility, but the job I really love is overseeing all the activities in the kitchen. You know, like testing all the food (which is really just tasting it), making suggestions for recipes, and best of all, eating all of the leftovers. The part about the leftovers truly makes life worth living!

Along with my ordinary duties I have other serious responsibilities. The human cook, Corrie, always makes me go with her during the berry-picking season. Corrie loops a rope around my neck and drags me all over the woods to pick berries. I squeal at the top of my lungs, which is just what she wants. It scares away the snakes.

If you'll promise not to tell the farm family, I'll let you in on a little secret. Once a month all the animals that live on the farm and around the river get together for a shindig that you wouldn't believe. (The farm family wouldn't believe it either.) We call it our Critter Cotillion.

On this special night, which is usually the third Saturday of every month, the food is plentiful and everyone has a fantastic time. Since I am in charge of food for the farm, I am also in charge of preparations for this get-together. All of the animals sort through their favorite recipes to find just the right one to share with the rest of us. Then I pick which recipes will go together the best. This is called "menu planning" and anybody can do it.

To Plan a Menu

Here's what you do:

Pick your main dish. This is usually a meat or some other hearty dish.

Then choose one or two side dishes made of vegetables, grains, or dairy products. Choose a bread and then a dessert or fruit dish to eat last. When planning your menu, remember if you choose colorful foods, the meal will look better and, most of all, taste better. Don't choose foods that are all the same color. Remember, a variety of color choosing one item from each of the four food groups can add taste and balance to your meal!

That's all there is to it. I've even put together some sample menus in the back of this book to help you get started.

But before we get started, you should know and follow these very important kitchen tips.

Before You Get Started

- Get permission from an adult, and ask an adult to help you in the kitchen. This is the most important step of all!
- Before going into the kitchen, wash your hands in warm soapy water and rinse them well. Then dry your hands thoroughly.
- Decide on your recipe.
- Read your recipe all the way through.
- Be sure you have all the ingredients before you start.
- Be sure your cooking area is clean, and be sure you keep it clean.
- Keep your clothes neat and clean anytime you cook. Do not wear clothing that has strings, fringes, or ruffles because they can catch on fire from the stove or oven.
- Be sure your hair is neatly fixed and does not come in contact with the food.

Safe Cooking Rules

- Always get your adult helper to handle pots when you are cooking on the stove, oven, or microwave.
- Be sure to use very thick oven mitts or pot holders when moving pots and pans.
- Be sure the handle of the pot is turned toward the center of the stove to keep it from spilling and to keep someone from bumping into it.
- Before you turn on the oven make sure the rack you are planning to use is placed in the center and do not allow pans in the oven to touch.
- Never place a hot pot directly on the kitchen counter. Place it on a pot holder or a trivet.
- Always be sure to turn off the stove burners and the oven when you finish cooking.
- When using a microwave oven, always follow the directions listed in the instruction book that came with your microwave. Never place any metal pots or pans in the microwave.

- Always get your adult helper if you are using electrical appliances such as mixers or toasters.
- Always dry your hands before plugging anything into an electrical outlet. This is very important so you don't get a shock.
- Never put your fingers into the bowl while the mixer motor is on. Be sure the mixer blades have stopped moving before you take a taste.
- Never pick up a knife by the blade. Pick it up only by the handle and keep the sharp edge facing down. When you're finished, lay the knife down flat on the table or counter.
- When using a vegetable peeler, be sure to peel away from yourself.

In Case of an Accident

- In case of a grease fire or small pan flames, place a lid over the flame to smother the fire or pour baking soda on the fire to smother it. Never pour water on a grease fire because it will cause the flames to spread.
- If you get cut or burned, call on your adult helper immediately.

Helpful Hints

- Measure carefully and follow directions.
- Wash and rinse the pots, pans, and bowls as you go along. This makes cleanup much easier.
- When you finish with an ingredient, put it back where it came from. This especially goes for meats and milk, butter, and other dairy products.

Measuring Up

3 teaspoons = 1 tablespoon
4 tablespoons = $\frac{1}{4}$ cup
5 tablespoons + 1 teaspoon = $\frac{1}{3}$ cup
8 tablespoons = $\frac{1}{2}$ cup
16 tablespoons = 1 cup
1 cup = 8 ounces
2 cups = 1 pint
2 pints = 1 quart
2 quarts = $\frac{1}{2}$ gallon
4 quarts = 1 gallon

Measuring Solids and Liquids

• Use the dry measuring cups for solid things such as sugar, flour, butter, and shortening. Make sure that you place your measuring cup on a flat surface. Fill the measuring cup until it is a little over the top, and then use a metal spatula to level it and scrape off any extra.
•When you measure very sticky things use a rubber spatula or a spoon to help scrape them out of the measuring cups.
•Use the measuring spoons for measuring very small amounts.
•Be sure to use a measuring cup that has a spout when you are measuring liquids. To make sure that you are measuring correctly, bend down so that your eyes are directly even with the level mark that you need on the side of the measuring cup.

Cooking Tools

Here are some of the utensils and equipment you'll be using to make your Critter Cakes, Frog Tea, and other treats.

rolling pin

baking sheet

sauce pans

spatula

baking pans

biscuit cutter

colander

cookie cutters

barbecue brush

vegetable peelers

sifter

egg beater

electric mixer

baking dish

frying pan

wire whisk

ice tray

grater

bowls

tea kettle

muffin tin

Now that you know some important things about being in the kitchen, let me share some things that are important to me—cooking and eating. Here are my favorite recipes.

Rooty Beggar Float

Makes 1 float

These floats are great after an afternoon of planting the garden or rolling in the mud.

Fixings
root beer
ice-cream

Cooking Tools
tall glass
ice cream scoop

Directions
1. Put 2 scoops of ice cream into glass.
2. Slowly pour root beer over ice cream.

Saturday Night Spaghetti

Makes 6 servings

All the animals love this dish, especially when they drop by on Saturday night for a game of cards.

Fixings
1 pound of ground beef
4 cups of water
2 (15-ounce) cans of tomato sauce
1 tablespoon of minced dried onion
3 shakes of salt
1 teaspoon of dried crushed oregano
1 teaspoon of Worcestershire sauce
1 teaspoon of sugar
$\frac{1}{2}$ teaspoon of dried, crushed basil
$\frac{1}{4}$ teaspoon of garlic powder
3 dashes of pepper
$\frac{1}{4}$ teaspoon of crushed dried parsley
1 (8-ounce) package of spaghetti noodles
$\frac{1}{2}$ cup of Parmesan cheese

Cooking Tools

4-quart saucepan with a lid
big wooden spoon
measuring spoons

Directions

1. Have an adult help you break the ground beef into a 4-quart saucepan, and put the pan on the stove over medium heat.
2. Constantly stir the meat with the wooden spoon to keep it from burning (it burns very easily). It's done when the pink color is gone.
3. Have your adult helper take the pan off the stove and spoon off the grease.
4. With the stove burner off, put the pan back on the stove and stir in the water, tomato sauce, dried onion, salt, oregano, Worcestershire sauce, sugar, basil, garlic, pepper, and dried parsley.
5. Turn the heat to high, and stir the mixture with the wooden spoon until it comes to a rolling boil (be careful and don't let it burn). Now break the spaghetti noodles into small pieces and put them into the pan with everything else.
6. Turn down the heat to low, put the lid on the pan, and stir the mixture every few minutes. It will take about 20 to 25 minutes for the noodles to cook.
7. Turn off the stove, and sprinkle the spaghetti with Parmesan cheese.

Stupendous Stuffers

Makes 4 servings
This dish has a lot of sentimental value for me because
Cleopatra used to prepare it when we were teenage piglets
and had just started dating. How romantic!

Fixings

2 quarts of water
4 jumbo shell noodles
1 (5-ounce) can of boneless chicken
2 tablespoons of light mayonnaise
mustard

$\frac{1}{4}$ teaspoon of salt
pepper
paprika
lettuce leaves

Cooking Tools

medium-sized saucepan
can opener
medium-sized mixing bowl

mixing spoon
serving dish
ice-cream scoop

Directions

1. Bring water to a boil in the saucepan.
2. Add the shell noodles to boiling water, and cook for 10 to 12 minutes or until tender. Ask your adult helper to stir the noodles while they are boiling so they won't stick together.
3. With a can opener open the can of chicken. Carefully pour off the liquid.
4. Put chicken in the mixing bowl.
5. While the noodles are cooking, combine the chicken, mayonnaise, mustard, salt, pepper,and paprika in the mixing bowl, and stir until blended.
6. Wash lettuce leaves, and arrange them in the bottom of the serving dish.
7. Drain the noodles, and put them into the serving dish.
8. Fill the ice-cream scoop half-full of chicken mixture, and stuff each noodle.
9. Place the stuffed noodles on the bed of lettuce in the serving dish.

Barbecued Baby Carrots

Makes 6 servings
These bite-sized morsels are sure to make even the most
serious of pigs squeal with delight.

Fixings

3 cups of baby carrots
barbecue sauce

Cooking Tools

paper towel
roasting pan with rack
barbecue brush

Directions

1. Preheat the oven to 325 degrees.
2. Wash the carrots, and dry them with a paper towel.
3. Place the carrots evenly on the rack of the roasting pan.
4. Carefully brush each carrot with barbecue sauce until thoroughly coated.
5. Bake for 45 minutes or until tender.

Veggy Bites

Cleopatra has been on a health food kick lately. (She's trying
to lose those unsightly hog jowls around her face.) This is
good for her hog jowls, and it's good for my taste buds.

Fixings

1 (10-ounce) package each
  of frozen broccoli florets
  and frozen cauliflower
1 pint of cherry tomatoes
4 tablespoons of Italian dressing
4 tablespoons Parmesan cheese

Cooking Tools

1 medium-sized saucepan
large serving bowl
mixing spoon
small mixing bowl
plastic wrap

Directions

1. Cook the broccoli and cauliflower in the saucepans according to the package directions.
2. While the broccoli and cauliflower are cooking, wash the cherry tomatoes.
3. Drain the broccoli and cauliflower, and combine them in the serving bowl.
4. Gently stir in the cherry tomatoes.
5. Combine the Italian dressing and Parmesan cheese in the mixing bowl until well blended.
6. Pour the dressing-and-cheese mixture over the broccoli and cauliflower, and stir gently.
7. Cover with plastic wrap, and chill in the refrigerator until you're ready to eat.

Red-Rip's Cornbread Muffins

Makes 12 muffins
These are the muffins my Mama used to make. They feel so good in my tummy, and they always bring back warm memories of my early pighood.

Fixings

vegetable oil
1 cup of cornmeal
1 cup of flour
$\frac{1}{2}$ teaspoon of salt
2 teaspoons of baking powder
1 egg
about 1 cup of milk
1 tablespoon of chopped, fresh chives

Cooking Tools

muffin tins
measuring cups
measuring spoons
mixing bowl
wooden spoon
paper towels

Directions

1. Preheat oven to 350 degrees.
2. Pour oil into muffin tins (just enough to cover the bottom), and have your adult helper put the muffin tins in the oven to let the oil get hot.
3. Mix the cornmeal, flour, salt, and baking powder together in the mixing bowl.
4. Beat in the egg with the wooden spoon and add to cornmeal mixture.
5. Add just enough milk to make a stiff batter.
6. Add the chopped chives.
7. Spoon the batter into the hot muffin tins, filling half-full, and bake for 25 minutes or until golden brown.
8. Drain the muffins on paper towels before serving.

Cinnamon-Sweet Coffeecake

Makes 8 servings

As you probably know, pigs don't like coffee. But coffeecake, well that's a different story. (Personally I don't like to take this to the Critter Cotillion because that means I have to share it.)

Fixings

Coffeecake:
2 cups of buttermilk baking mix
$\frac{2}{3}$ cup of milk
2 tablespoons of sugar
2 tablespoons of cinnamon
1 egg
cooking spray

Topping:
$\frac{1}{3}$ cup of baking mix
$\frac{1}{3}$ cup of packed brown sugar
$\frac{1}{2}$ teaspoons of cinnamon
2 tablespoons of butter

Cooking Tools

medium-sized mixing bowl
mixing spoon
small mixing bowl

9-inch round baking pan coated with shortening or cooking spray

Directions

1. Preheat oven to 350 degrees.
2. Mix coffeecake ingredients in medium-sized mixing bowl, and beat with the spoon for 1 minute.
3. Spread batter in baking pan.
4. Mix topping ingredients in a small mixing bowl until crumbly.
5. Sprinkle topping over batter.
6. Bake for 18 to 22 minutes.
7. Serve warm.

Red-Rip's Snapdoodle

Makes 1 cake
This is a wonderful afternoon snack.

Fixings

$\frac{1}{2}$ cup of shortening
1 cup of sugar
3 cups of all-purpose flour
$\frac{1}{2}$ teaspoon of salt
1 teaspoon of baking powder
1 $\frac{1}{2}$ cups of milk
1 $\frac{1}{2}$ cups of brown sugar, packed
$\frac{1}{8}$ teaspoon of cinnamon
$\frac{1}{8}$ teaspoon of mace

Cooking Tools

measuring spoons
measuring cups
2 medium-sized mixing bowls
1 small mixing bowl
13 x 9 x 2-inch baking pan coated
with shortening or vegetable
cooking spray
mixing spoon
knife

Directions

1. Preheat oven to 350 degrees.
2. Combine shortening and sugar in a mixing bowl, and cream until the mixture is fluffy.
3. In another mixing bowl, combine the flour, salt, and baking powder.

4. Add the flour mixture to the sugar mixture alternately (taking turns) with the milk, and mix well.
5. Pour the batter into the baking pan.
6. Combine the brown sugar, cinnamon, and mace in a small bowl. Mix well, and sprinkle over the top of the batter.
7. Bake for about 50 minutes or until brown.
8. Cut it into squares after it cools.

Red-Rip's Bumpy Brownies

Makes 32 brownies
Chopped walnuts make the tops of these brownies look like
the rocky road down to our pond.

Fixings

1 cup of semisweet chocolate chips
2 $\frac{1}{2}$ tablespoons of butter, cut into bits
1 large egg
$\frac{1}{4}$ cup of sugar
$\frac{1}{2}$ teaspoon of pure vanilla
pinch of salt
2 tablespoons of all-purpose flour
$\frac{1}{2}$ cup of chopped walnuts

Cooking Tools

heavy saucepan
measuring spoons
measuring cups
wooden spoon
small mixing bowl
whisk
8-inch square pan coated with butter and floured

Directions

1. Preheat oven to 350 degrees.
2. Put ¾ cup of chocolate chips and butter in top of heavy saucepan and melt over very low heat, being careful not to burn, stirring until the mixture is smooth.
3. In the small bowl whisk together the egg, sugar, and vanilla until the mixture is foamy.
4. Whisk in the chocolate mixture and a pinch of salt, whisking until smooth.
5. Fold in the flour and the remaining ¼ cup of chocolate chips and the walnuts.
6. Spoon the batter into the pan.
7. Bake for 15 to 20 minutes.
8. Let cool for 15 to 20 minutes and cut into squares.

Now let me introduce a few of my friends so they can share their favorite recipes and fun things to do in the kitchen.

MR. FROG

First, allow me to introduce Mr. Frog. He's the guy sitting over there on the lily pad. Mr. Frog is a retired judge, and he's an immaculate dresser. (Yes, even pigs notice those things!) Just look at him. He's wearing his favorite outfit—a beautiful persimmon-colored silk vest, purple trousers, a pearl-gray jacket, and of course, his gold watch. The gold watch chain across his stomach shows off the engraved gavel on his watch fob. He got that gavel for being the best judge who ever sat on the bench in Emerald River County. His grandfather told him that there are certain things that make a gentleman, and that a gold watch is one of them. Even though he's a gentleman, Mr. Frog's not so bad. He is a pillar of the community and one of the smartest lawyers to graduate from Emerald University. (I know all of this is true because Mr. Frog told me himself.)

Mr. Frog's favorite pastime is sitting on that lily pad in the duck pond and eating his lunch. Occasionally Mr. Frog brings out one of his scrumptious cucumber-and-radish tea sandwiches. Because he knows how much the ducks, Que and Quan, enjoy cucumbers, Mr. Frog nibbles slowly and deliberately licks his lips. Que and Quan constantly try to eat those cool green cucumbers. When they simply can't watch him eat any longer, they dive under the water and thump his lily pad, making Mr. Frog lose his balance. Down he'll go with his cucumber-and-radish sandwich. What a sight to see the dignified Mr. Frog crawl out of the pond, with his wet skin sagging, and head for his hammock!

Mr. Frog retired some time ago, but that doesn't keep him from exerting his influence whenever he wants to, which is most of the time. Lucky for us, being retired doesn't keep him from making the best teatime around either. There's nothing quite like Mr. Frog's Gooey Fruities and Sour Cream Tea Biscuits. Yum-yum.

Mr. Frog would like to tell you some important things about manners before he shares his best teatime recipes with you.

Mr. Frog's Words That Work Magic

 These words can help even the most undignified animal handle a situation properly and with grace. These words helped make me the Frog I am today. Always use these words, and they will work magic for you, too!

THANK YOU! You should always show your appreciation to others.

EXCUSE ME! Ask to be excused when you need to leave the table or whenever you bump into someone or, heaven forbid, interrupt someone else when they're speaking.

I'M SORRY! Wonderful words to use whenever you have done something that upsets or hurts someone else. These words are truly magic when they are said from the heart.

PLEASE! This magic word placed in front of any request makes it much more likely that you will get what you ask for.

YOU'RE WELCOME! Always reply with these magic words whenever someone says thank you.

I LOVE YOU! The most magical of all words, these can be substituted for any of the above and should be said often.

Frog Tea

A tea party is a magical thing with sweet treats that glitter like jewels—ready to be picked. Tea, of course, is essential to every tea party. Here's how to make the very best tea, guaranteed to impress your guests.

Fixings

1 teaspoon loose tea leaves or 1 teaspoon per cup of water
sugar
thin slices of fresh lemon
heavy cream
milk

Cooking Tools

kettle
teacups
teapot

Directions

1. Fill the kettle with cold water.
2. Ask your adult helper to place the kettle on the stove over high heat.
3. When the water is barely boiling, pour a little into the teapot.
4. Stir it around to warm the pot, and then pour it out.
5. Put the tea leaves into the teapot. The old way was to use 1 teaspoon of leaves for each person plus 1 teaspoon for the pot.
6. Take the teapot to the kettle, and just as soon as the kettle starts to boil, have your adult helper pour the water over the tea leaves.
7. Then put the lid on the teapot, and let it simmer for 3 to 5 minutes.
8. When the tea is ready, serve it on a tray with teacups, sugar, lemon, cream, and milk.
9. Pour each guest's cup of tea, after politely asking whether he or she would prefer sugar, lemon, cream or milk.

Mr. Frog's Cucumber-and-Radish Tea Sandwiches

Makes 40 small sandwiches
These are so pretty, with the little bits of red radishes peeping out.
They are easy to make and quite scrumptious. No wonder the ducks,
Que and Quan, constantly try to sneak them from my lily pad.

Fixings

2 medium-sized fresh cucumbers
vinegar
salt
white pepper
10 slices of white bread
½ cup of softened butter
1 bunch of red radishes

Cooking Tools

paring knife
measuring spoons
medium-sized china bowl
(do not use an aluminum bowl)
butter knife
colander or strainer
paper towels

Directions

1. Wash the cucumbers, and then cut them into thin slices.
2. Put the cucumber slices in a shallow china bowl (never use an aluminum bowl for cucumbers).
3. Sprinkle them with vinegar and a dash of salt and white pepper, and leave them for about 1 hour.
4. Trim the crust from each slice of bread, and spread butter on each side.
5. Cut each piece of bread into four equal squares.
6. Drain the cucumber slices, and dry them on paper towels. Then layer them on half of the squares of bread.
7. Wash the radishes, dry them on paper towels, and then cut them into thin slices.
8. Overlap the cucumber with red radish circles so that red edges show at the edge of the bread.
9. Top with the remaining squares of bread, and gently press the two halves together.

Froggy Carrot Salad

Makes 6 servings
My secret recipe for this cool salad makes me the envy of all
the animals on the Emerald River. It is, of course, a favorite
at our Critter Cotillion.

Fixings

4 medium carrots
1 (8-ounce) can of crushed pineapple
$\frac{1}{2}$ cup of raisins
$\frac{1}{4}$ cup of mayonnaise

Cooking Tools

vegetable peeler
grater
medium-sized mixing bowl

Directions

1. Wash carrots well and peel them.
2. Grate the carrots into a mixing bowl.
3. Drain the pineapple and add it to the carrots.
4. Stir in the raisins and mayonnaise and mix well.
5. Refrigerate the mixture until it is chilled.

Gooey Fruities

Makes 8 servings
This fruit topping is perfect to dress up my Sour Cream Tea
Biscuits. I love to serve these when faculty members from
Emerald University come to my lily pad for tea.

Fixings

$\frac{1}{3}$ cup of fruit preserves
(pear and peach are excellent!)
1 stick of softened butter
a pinch of powdered sugar
$\frac{1}{2}$ teaspoon of lemon juice

Cooking Tools

mixing spoon
mixing bowl
pretty serving dish

Directions

1. Combine preserves, butter, powdered sugar, and lemon juice in a small mixing bowl, and stir until well mixed.
2. Serve in the crock as a spread for tea biscuits or toast.
3. Store leftover mixture in an airtight container in the refrigerator.

Mr. Frog's Sour Cream Tea Biscuits

Makes 16 biscuits

My Sour Cream Tea Biscuits are a favorite at the high teas that I serve for members of the faculty of Emerald University. Red-Rip likes to tell the story about the morning I asked Robin Rat to pick up some sour cream for me at the store because I was so busy getting ready for all my guests. I gave Robin Rat enough money to buy it and told her, "Now Robin, be sure it's fresh." "Fresh?" answered Rat. "How can it be fresh when it is already sour?"

Fixings

2 cups of all-purpose flour
1 teaspoon of double-acting baking powder
2 teaspoons of sugar
½ teaspoon of baking soda
½ teaspoon of salt
6 tablespoons of cold vegetable shortening
brush
½ cup of sour cream
½ cup of club soda
2 tablespoons of butter, melted
1 cup of chopped, fresh parsley

Cooking Tools

large mixing bowl
measuring cups
measuring spoons
flour sifter
large mixing spoon
small mixing bowl
small round cookie cutter
9-inch baking pan coated with shortening or cooking spray
serving platter

Directions

1. Preheat oven to 400 degrees.
2. In a large mixing bowl, sift together flour, baking powder, sugar, baking soda , and salt. Cut in the shortening until the mixture looks like coarse meal.
3. Stir together the sour cream and club soda in the small bowl.
4. Add the sour cream mixture to the flour mixture, stirring until the mixture forms a soft dough.
5. Form the dough into a ball, and pat out to 1-inch thickness on a floured surface.
6. Cut out the biscuits with the cookie cutter and arrange them in the baking pan.
7. Brush the tops with melted butter, and bake on middle rack for 20 to 25 minutes.
8. Transfer biscuits to a wire rack, and brush with melted butter. Place the biscuits on a serving platter and surround with fresh parsley.

Popovers That Really Pop Over

Makes 6 servings

Fixings

1 cup of all-purpose flour
$\frac{1}{4}$ teaspoon of salt
$\frac{3}{4}$ cup of milk, plus a little extra
2 eggs
$\frac{1}{2}$ teaspoon of melted butter

Cooking Tools

flour sifter
mixing bowl
measuring cups

measuring spoons
small saucepan
egg beater
about 8 muffin tins or custard cups coated with shortening or vegetable
  cooking spray
large spoon

Directions

1. Preheat oven to 450 degrees.
2. Sift together flour and salt into a mixing bowl.
3. Add the milk gradually to make a paste.
4. Beat the eggs until light, and add them to the batter.
5. Add the melted butter.
6. Fill muffin tins two-thirds full, and bake for 10 minutes.
7. Lower heat to 350 degrees, and bake 30 minutes longer.

Heavenly Bits

Makes 12 cookies
These thumb-size cookies are my teatime favorites.

Fixings

1 stick of softened butter
2 tablespoons of sugar
1 cup of self-rising flour
1 teaspoon of vanilla
1 cup of finely chopped pecans
powdered sugar

Cooking Tools

1 medium-sized mixing bowl
aluminum foil

baking sheet covered with aluminum foil
measuring cups
measuring spoons

Directions

1. Preheat oven to 325 degrees.
2. Mix together the butter, sugar, flour, vanilla, and chopped pecans. The dough will be crumbly.
3. Take a small amount of dough in your hand, and roll it into small balls.
4. Put cookies on the baking sheet, and bake for about 20 minutes.
5. While the cookies are still warm, roll them in powdered sugar.

Mr. Frog's Favorite Fruit Dip

Makes ¾ cup of dip
This dip is wonderful with apple and banana slices and orange sections. I used to really enjoy this as a pick-me-up snack during my long days in law school at Emerald University.

Fixings

½ cup of peanut butter
¼ cup of chocolate syrup or honey
fresh fruit

Cooking Tools

mixing spoon
small mixing bowl

Directions

1. Combine the peanut butter and chocolate syrup or honey in a mixing bowl, and stir until well mixed.
2. Dip in pieces of fresh fruit.

ROBIN RAT

Early each day a little brown face with long whiskers, thick silky hair, and tiny ears appears at the edge of the duck pond. It belongs to Robin Rat.

Robin's little house is on the bank of the duck pond, and Que and Quan are nice enough to allow her swimming privileges most of the time.

Sometimes the ducks do object to Robin swimming, because when they stand on their heads suddenly (as ducks often do) she likes to tickle the bottoms of their feet, causing them to suddenly pop their heads back out of the water. By the time the ducks climb out of the pond spitting and shaking their feathers in anger, Robin has disappeared.

As you can see, Robin is a very mischievous little rat, but, boy, can she cook! She also makes her own bubble-blowing solution so that we can have fun at the Critter Cotillion. Here she is to tell you how she does it.

Robin Rat's Bubble-Blowing Solution

This is not for eating or drinking.
You and your friends will have fun with this, and it's so easy to make! Try it at your next birthday party.
It was a hit at mine.

Fixings

1 $\frac{1}{4}$ cups of water
$\frac{1}{3}$ cup of no-tear baby shampoo
2 teaspoons of sugar
2 drops of food coloring

Cooking Tools

plastic airtight container with a screw-on lid

Directions

1. Put all ingredients into the container and securely fasten lid.
2. Shake well.
3. Use the mixture to blow bubbles.

Homemade Milkshakes

Makes 1 shake
Like most river rats, I have a sweet tooth. My favorite way to satisfy it is with ice cream. You can join me with these creamy homemade shakes.

Fixings

your favorite flavor ice cream
2 tablespoons of chocolate syrup
4 ounces of milk

Cooking Tools

tall glass
mixing spoon

Directions

1. Put 2 scoops of ice cream into the glass.
2. Pour the chocolate syrup over the ice cream.
3. Add the milk, and mix well with a spoon.

Wowsie Wingers!

Makes 6 servings
These wingers make a humdinger of a snack or a yummy (but messy) main dish for dinner.

Fixings

1 package of fresh mini-chicken legs
barbecue sauce
ranch-style salad dressing

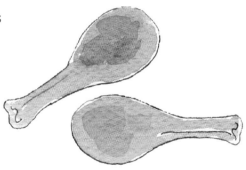

Cooking Tools

roasting pan with rack
barbecue brush

Directions

1. Preheat oven to 325 degrees.
2. Arrange the chicken legs on the rack of the roasting pan.
3. Coat both sides of each chicken leg with barbecue sauce using the brush.
4. Bake for 30 minutes or until tender.
5. Dip in ranch dressing for extra flavor.

Eggstras

Makes 6 servings
The perfect side dish for Wowsie Wingers!—and just about everything else.

Fixings

3 eggs
1 tablespoon of mayonnaise
$\frac{1}{4}$ tablespoon of spicy mustard
1 tablespoon of pickle relish
salt
pepper

Cooking Tools

large saucepan with lid
knife
mixing bowl
mixing spoon
serving plate

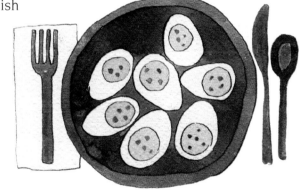

Directions

1. Place eggs in saucepan, and cover with water.
2. Put lid on pan, and bring water to boil.
3. Have your adult helper take the pan off the stove immediately, and let it stand for 15 minutes.
4. Drain eggs, and rinse with cold water.
5. Peel the eggs and cut each one in half (ask an adult to help).
6. Take out the yellow egg yolks and put them into the mixing bowl.
7. Add mayonnaise, mustard, pickle relish, and a sprinkle of salt and pepper to egg yolks, and mix well.
8. Arrange the egg halves in a circle on the serving plate, and spoon the yolk mixture into the hole of each egg half.

Green Stuff

Makes 6 servings

This sweet salad is a favorite at our Critter Cotillion. I never have leftovers when I bring it! The raccoon twins, Roscoe and Sweet William, say it makes them play sweet music on their fiddles.

Fixings

1 (8-ounce) can of crushed pineapple
one package of instant pistachio pudding mix
8 ounces of whipped topping
1 $\frac{1}{2}$ cups of mini-marshmallows

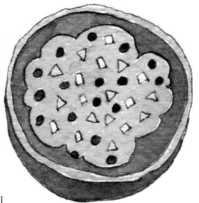

Cooking Tools

serving bowl
mixing spoon

Directions

1. Drain the pineapple, and put it into the bowl.
2. Sprinkle the pudding mix over the pineapple.
3. Stir in the whipped topping and the mini-marshmallows, and mix well.

Yummy Cheese Biscuits

Makes 16 biscuits

My most famous culinary achievement. This is what good little rats get to eat, and bad little rats can only dream about.

Fixings

2 cups of flour
1 tablespoon of double-acting baking powder
1 teaspoon of sugar

½ teaspoon of salt
⅓ cup of grated cheddar cheese
5 tablespoons of butter, cut into small pieces
1 tablespoon of grated Parmesan cheese
¾ cup of milk
paprika

Cooking Tools

large mixing bowl
flour sifter
measuring spoons
measuring cups
rolling pin
1 ½-inch biscuit cutter
baking sheet coated with shortening or cooking spray

Directions

1. Preheat oven to 400 degrees.
2. In large mixing bowl, sift together flour, baking powder, sugar, and salt.
3. Add cheddar cheese, butter, and Parmesan cheese.
4. Add milk and stir just enough to make a soft, smooth dough.
5. Turn the dough out onto a floured surface, and knead it for a few seconds (get your adult helper to show you how to knead).
6. Sprinkle the dough with a little flour, and roll it out to ⅓-inch thickness.
7. Cut out small biscuits with cutter.
8. Arrange biscuits on baking sheet about 1 inch apart.
9. Bake for 12 to 15 minutes or until golden brown.
10. Sprinkle tops of biscuits with paprika.

Tomato Toasties

Makes 1 sandwich
I love this sandwich—it's so quick and easy and good to eat
on cool days!

Fixings

1 slice of bread
1 slice of cheddar cheese
1 slice of tomato

Cooking Tools

baking sheet

Directions

1. Preheat oven to 300 degrees.
2. Place the bread slice on baking sheet.
3. Put the cheese slice on top of the bread.
4. Put the tomato slice in the center of the cheese slice.
5. Bake until the cheese begins to brown. Be sure to ask your adult helper to take the baking sheet out of the oven.

Cherry Whiff

Makes 6 servings
This is called "whiff" because when I smell it baking, my
nose "whiffs " up and down. Mmm!

Fixings

¾ cup of sugar
¼ cup of sifted all-purpose flour
1 (10-ounce) can of sour red cherries in juice
1 can of biscuits
2 tablespoons of butter

Cooking Tools

saucepan
measuring cups
wooden spoon
8-inch square baking dish
knife

Directions

1. Preheat oven to 425 degrees.
2. Blend ½ cup of sugar and the flour together in the saucepan.
3. Have your adult helper add the juice from the canned cherries and help
   you cook the mixture over medium heat. Stir constantly until thickened.
4. Add the cherries.
5. Spoon the cherry mixture into the baking dish, and stir well.
6. Open the can of biscuits and cut each biscuit in half. Place the biscuits
   (cut side down) on top of the cherries, and dot with butter.
7. Sprinkle the remaining ¼ cup of sugar on top of the butter and bake for
   15 to 20 minutes or until the crust is nicely browned
8. If you have any ice cream, top your whiff with a glob!

Fruitysicles

Makes 8 Fruitysicles

These are great for those sunshiny days when I lounge on my raft in the duck pond. I can enjoy my fruitysicle and tickle the ducks' feet at the same time!

Fixings

your favorite fruit juice (orange, grape, and cranberry all make tasty
  Fruitysicles)

Cooking Tools

6-ounce paper cups
plastic wrap
popsicle sticks

Directions

1. Pour fruit juice into the cups.
2. Cover the top of each cup with plastic wrap.
3. Poke a popsicle stick through the center of the plastic wrap into each cup.
4. Put the cups into the freezer.
5. After your Fruitysicles are frozen, serve them by taking off the plastic wrap and pulling them out of the cup!

QUE & QUAN THE DUCKS

Que and Quan are a pair of beautiful Peking ducks. They are the walking newspaper for all the animals. Their favorite pastime is gossip! They like to walk around and visit with the other animals that live close to their pond. When they're not gossiping or visiting, you can be sure they're either eating or taking a nap.

All the animals know the importance of staying on good terms with the ducks. Que, the male duck, is usually nice, but he will square off and fight if uninvited guests invade the pond or the corn bin. He isn't really mean, he just likes to hiss and quack a lot, but most of the animals try to keep him from doing that!

Quan, on the other hand, is always gracious and kind. That's why they make such a perfect couple—they balance each other.

Sometimes they try to sneak up to the raccoon twins' place and eat the cherries that have fallen off the beautiful cherry tree in the backyard. Sweet William often shares, but Roscoe always says, "There is an old saying: The way to keep milk fresh is to keep it in the cow. So the way to keep my cherries is to keep them on the tree."

Both Que and Quan are good cooks. Here they are to share some of the recipes they like to show off at our monthly Critter Cotillion.

39

Nutter Cones

This is for the birds to eat, not for people. These make a great snack for any birds that live around your house.

Fixings

1 large pinecone
peanut butter
birdseed

Cooking Tools

waxed paper
butter knife
fishing line

Directions

1. Stand up the pinecone in the center of a piece of waxed paper.
2. Using a butter knife, spread peanut butter on the ends of the pinecone.
3. Sprinkle birdseed on the peanut butter.
4. Tie fishing line around the top of the pinecone so that it hangs straight.
5. Hang your nutter cone outside for the birds to enjoy.

Pond Water

Makes 5 8-ounce cups
The color of this drink will remind you of our lovely home.

Fixings

$\frac{1}{2}$ cup of hot water
$\frac{1}{2}$ cup of sugar
$\frac{1}{2}$ cup of lemon or lime juice
4 cups of cold water
ice cubes
lemon or lime slices

Cooking Tools

glass or plastic pitcher
mixing spoon

Directions

1. Pour hot water into pitcher.
2. Add sugar, and stir until dissolved.
3. Stir in the juice and cold water.
4. Add the ice cubes, and garnish with lemon or lime slices.

Toad in the Hole

Makes 6 servings

We ducks love anything with spicy meat! This old-fashioned sausage pie recipe is a good choice for breakfast, brunch, or Sunday-night supper.

Fixings

12 link sausages
3 eggs
1 cup of milk
1 cup of sifted flour
1 teaspoon of salt
a sprinkle of pepper
applesauce (optional)

Cooking Tools

medium-sized skillet
spatula
2-quart casserole dish
large mixing bowl
measuring spoons
measuring cups
mixing spoon
paring knife

Directions

1. Preheat oven to 400 degrees.
2. Put the sausages in the skillet and cover them with cold water.
3. Brown the sausages on all sides using a spatula to turn them as they cook.
4. Ask your adult helper to pour off some of the fat, and then transfer the sausages to the casserole dish.
5. Blend the 3 eggs with the milk, flour, salt, and a sprinkle of pepper in the mixing bowl, and mix until smooth.

6. Pour the batter over the sausages, and bake for 35 minutes or until the top is puffed and browned.
7. Cut into wedges, and serve at once. It's delicious with applesauce!

Que and Quan's Corn Pudding

Makes 6 servings
Ducks do like to fuss and make noise, but in our quieter moments, we make this recipe with our favorite food—corn!

Fixings

½ cup of milk
2 tablespoons of melted butter
1 teaspoon of salt
2 tablespoons of all-purpose flour
1 tablespoon of soy sauce
2 cups of cream-style corn (canned)
1 well-beaten egg
soft bread crumbs, buttered
¼ cup of finely chopped fresh parsley for topping

Cooking Tools

medium-sized mixing bowl
large mixing spoon
1 ½ quart casserole dish coated with shortening or cooking spray.
measuring spoons
measuring cups

Directions

1. Preheat oven to 350 degrees.
2. Combine milk, butter, salt, flour, soy sauce, corn, and egg in a mixing bowl and mix well.

3. Pour the mixture into the casserole dish, sprinkle with bread crumbs, and bake for 30 minutes or until firm.
4. Sprinkle fresh parsley over top just before serving.

A small snippet of fresh dill makes the pudding even more delicious.

Bird Nests

Makes 8 servings
When we invite guests for early morning tea, this is what we ducks serve. It's also a good snack or side dish for any old time.

Fixings

instant grits
hot water
grated cheese or bacon bits
butter

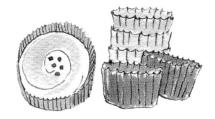

Cooking Tools

spoon
paper muffin cups

Directions

1. Mix grits with water according to the package directions. (Make sure they're not runny.)
2. Spoon grits to fill muffin cups three-quarters full.
3. Using the back of the spoon or your thumb, make an indention in the center of the grits, and sprinkle in grated cheese or bacon bits.
4. Dot butter on top of cheese or bacon bits.

Nutty Nanner Bread

Makes 1 loaf
This is a favorite of Que, who always says, "I love bananas because they don't have bones." You can serve this with cream cheese on top if you want to.

Fixings

2 cups of all-purpose flour
$\frac{3}{4}$ teaspoons of baking soda
salt
$\frac{1}{2}$ cup (1 stick) of butter, at room temperature
$\frac{3}{4}$ cup of sugar
2 eggs
3 very ripe bananas
2 tablespoons of sour cream
1 cup of chopped walnuts
cream cheese spread (optional)

Cooking Tools

measuring cups
measuring spoons
small mixing bowl
wooden spoon
large mixing bowl
electric mixer
loaf pan 8 $\frac{1}{2}$ x 4 $\frac{1}{2}$-inch coated with shortening or cooking spray
knife

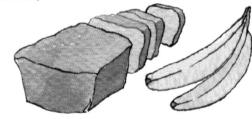

Directions

1. Preheat oven to 350 degrees.
2. Mix flour, baking soda, and salt in the small mixing bowl with the wooden spoon.

3. Put the butter and sugar in the large mixing bowl, and beat with the electric mixer until the mixture is pale yellow and creamy.
4. Add the eggs to the butter mixture, and beat until completely blended.
5. Add the flour mixture, and beat until smooth.
6. Peel the bananas, and cut into large chunks.
7. Add the bananas and sour cream to the batter, and mix until smooth.
8. Add walnuts, and mix until evenly distributed.
9. Pour the batter into the loaf pan, and bake for about 1 hour and 10 minutes. The bread must shrink away from the sides—if not, bake for another 10 minutes.
10. Let the bread cool for 15 minutes before turning it out of the pan.
11. Set the bread right side up, and let it cool for another 15 minutes.

Cinnamon-Sugary Toast

This is a duck's delight

Fixings

2 slices of white bread
butter
1 teaspoon of cinnamon
1 teaspoon of sugar

Cooking Tools

toaster
butter knife

Directions

1. Lightly toast bread in the toaster.
2. Butter the bread immediately after it pops up.
3. Sprinkle with cinnamon and sugar.

Lemon Buttercups

Makes 6 servings
Quan makes this elegant little snack when special guests
come to visit at the pond. (It's also nice when it's garnished
with a couple of lemon drops or a slice of lime.)

Fixings

1 package of lemon pudding mix
bread slices (one piece of bread for each muffin cup in tin)
1 teaspoon of butter per bread slice

Cooking Tools

butter knife
muffin tins
mixing spoon

Directions

1. Preheat oven to 375 degrees.
2. Prepare lemon pudding according to package directions.
3. While pudding is chilling, trim the crusts off each slice of bread.
4. Butter bread on one side.
5. With buttered side down, press the bread gently into the muffin cups, folding or lapping the sides when needed.
6. Bake for 10 minutes, and let cool.
7. When pudding is chilled, spoon into the "buttercups" and serve.

Persnickety Popcorn

Makes 8 cups
What a great feast for us ducks and for you! Quan makes this
to supplement our corn and saves it in an airtight container
to enjoy any time.

Fixings

microwave popcorn
seasoning salt

Cooking Tools

large serving bowl

Directions

1. Pop the popcorn in microwave according to package directions.
2. Carefully open the popcorn bag (it's hot!), and sprinkle in 2 shakes of seasoning salt.
3. Close the bag, and shake well.
4. Repeat steps 2 and 3.
5. Pour seasoned popcorn into the bowl.

ROSCOE & SWEET WILLIAM
THE TWIN RACCOONS

The identical twin raccoons, Roscoe and Sweet William, have little iron-gray bodies and inquisitive black-masked faces. There's only one way to tell them apart: Roscoe always has a fierce look on his face, and Sweet William has a sweet look, like his name.

The raccoons were found under a palmetto tree after a bad storm and were brought to the farm by one of the farmhands. Now they live in a secluded clump of trees.

Sweet William quickly made friends with the other animals. But Roscoe worries about the other animals stealing his food, especially the cherries from the beautiful cherry tree in his backyard.

On a soft summer evening there is nothing more pleasant than to sit back and listen to Sweet William and Roscoe as they play their fiddles out under that cherry tree.

The raccoons' favorite time of the year is late October, when Indian summer ends. The cool, crisp air reminds the raccoons that it's time to go into the countryside and find wild persimmons.

Roscoe and Sweet William chant this old folk rhyme as they make their way to the woods:

Possum up the 'simmon tree,
Raccoon on the ground.
Raccoon says, "You son of a gun!
Shake those 'simmons down!

When they get to the woods they gather many baskets of bright orange persimmons. They are very careful not to put too many in each basket because persimmons bruise very easily. The Critter Cotillion in October after 'simmon gathering is always a good-eating time, thanks to Roscoe and Sweet William.

Because they are so good with their hands, the raccoons are also our experts on setting the table. Here they are with some good advice—and their yummiest recipes!

Setting the Table

We enjoy eating, and we always enjoy it more when the table looks nice. Here's how we make it look wonderful.

1. Clean off the table.
2. Cover the table with a tablecloth or lay down a place mat for each person who will be eating.
3. Put plates in front of each chair, or in the center of each place mat.
4. To the right of each plate, place a knife, with the sharp edge facing toward the plate.
5. Place the spoon on the right of the knife.
6. Set the glass on the right of the plate above the knife and the spoon.
7. Fold the napkin in half and place it to the left of the plate.
8. Place the fork on top of the napkin.
9. For a centerpiece, you can put flowers, fruit, nuts or whatever you like best in the center of the table.

Cherry Icers

Makes 1 ice tray of cube
We raccoons pick fresh cherries off our
treat. Cherry Icers add a yummy twist

Fixings

water
maraschino cherries

Cooking Tools

ice tray

Directions

1. Fill the ice tray with water.
2. Put a cherry in each section of the tray, making sure the stem is sticking out of the water.
3. Put the tray in the freezer until the water is frozen.
4. Empty the ice tray, and drop the Cherry Icers into your favorite drink.

Secret Hamburgers

Makes 6 hamburgers
Raccoons like these as much as kids do!

Fixings

1 ½ pounds of ground beef
¼ cup of dry bread crumbs
¼ cup of finely chopped onion
1 egg
1 teaspoon of salt
1 teaspoon of Worcestershire sauce
¼ teaspoon of white pepper
6 dill pickle slices

51

Tools

ing bowl
g knife
uring spoons
suring cups
iling pan
atula

Directions

1. Put the ground beef, bread crumbs, onion, egg, salt, Worcestershire sauce, and white pepper in a large mixing bowl, and blend well.
2. Shape the mixture into 12 thin patties (about 4" in diameter).
3. Put 1 dill pickle slice in the center of each of the six patties.
4. Top each with another patty (the pickle slice will be hidden inside), and press around the edge of each patty to seal.
5. Have your adult helper broil the patties for about 5 minutes on each side.

Stuffed Round-Rosy Apples

Makes 6 servings
We raccoons love fruit, and we always wash it in the river before we eat it. Be sure to wash your apples before you make this lip-smacking anytime treat.

Fixings

6 baking apples
3 cups of orange juice
1 tablespoon of grated, fresh orange peel
1 $\frac{1}{2}$ cups of brown sugar
butter
$\frac{1}{8}$ teaspoon of cinnamon

Cooking Tools
knife
scoop
measuring cups
measuring spoons
mixing bowl
baking dish coated with shortening or cooking spray

Directions
1. Heat oven to 375 degrees.
2. Cut each of the apples in half lengthwise, and scoop out the cores.
3. Combine the orange juice, orange peel, and 1 $\frac{1}{2}$ cups brown sugar.
4. Fill the apples with $\frac{3}{4}$ cup of brown sugar mixture, and spread the remainder of the mixture in the bottom of the baking dish.
5. Arrange the filled apples in the baking dish, and dot them with butter.
6. Bake for 30 minutes, basting frequently with the orange juice syrup.
7. Sprinkle with cinnamon, and serve hot.

Little Cabbages
Makes 6 servings
This is a special treat for us. Brussels sprouts, which look like little cabbages, are hardly bigger than rosebuds and have beautiful petals! Mmm, they taste good, too!

Fixings
$\frac{1}{2}$ cup of butter
1 small onion, chopped
2 pints of freshly washed brussels sprouts
2 tablespoons of water

Cooking Tools
heavy saucepan with lid
measuring cups
measuring spoons

Directions
1. Melt the butter in the saucepan and sauté (simmer) the chopped onion for 2 to 3 minutes until it is soft but not brown.
2. Add brussels sprouts and 2 tablespoons of water.
3. Cover the saucepan with a lid, and cook until the brussels sprouts are done but not mushy.

Party Biscuits a la Roscoe

Makes 14 biscuits
There is much to be said for a flaky golden biscuit, freshly baked,
and spread with melting butter. Roscoe makes the best biscuits
in Emerald River.

Fixings
2 cups of self-rising flour
1 teaspoon of salt
$\frac{1}{4}$ cup of shortening
$\frac{3}{4}$ cup of buttermilk

Cooking Tools
mixing bowl
large wooden spoon
measuring spoons
measuring cups
rolling pin
1-inch biscuit cutter
baking sheet coated with shortening or
cooking spray

Directions

1. Preheat oven to 400 degrees.
2. Mix the flour and salt in the bowl, mixing well.
3. Cut in the shortening until the mixture looks like coarse meal.
4. Stir in buttermilk, and knead the dough lightly 3 or 4 times (get your adult helper to show you how to knead).
5. Turn the dough out onto a floured surface, and roll it out to about ½-inch thickness.
6. Cut out biscuits with biscuit cutter.
7. Place on baking sheet and bake for 10 to 12 minutes.

Razzle-Dazzle Blueberry Muffins

Makes 14 muffins

These will dazzle your guests (if you haven't already eaten them all yourself). Remember, serve others before you serve yourself!

Fixings

1 cup of all-purpose flour
1 cup of yellow cornmeal
1 teaspoon of salt
1 tablespoon of double-acting baking powder
½ cup of butter, melted
⅓ cup of sugar
⅓ cup of honey
1 large egg
¾ cup of milk
2 cups of fresh blueberries

Cooking Tools

measuring cups
measuring spoons

large mixing bowl
small mixing bowl
whisk
wooden spoon
12 small muffin tins coated with shortening or cooking spray
wire rack

Directions

1. Preheat oven to 425 degrees.
2. Combine the flour, cornmeal, salt, and baking powder in the large mixing bowl.
3. In the small bowl, whisk together melted butter, sugar, honey, egg, and milk.
4. Add the butter mixture to the flour mixture, stirring to combine. Gently stir in the blueberries.
5. Spoon the mixture into the muffin tins, and bake on the middle rack for 15 to 20 minutes.
6. Let cool on a wire rack.

Peachy Peach Cobbler

Makes 8 servings
As Mr. Frog always says, "Cooking by guess is sure to result in a mess!" Measure carefully when you follow this recipe, and you will have the most delicious dessert ever.

Fixings

4 cups of sliced fresh peaches
1 ½ cups of water
1 ¼ cups of sugar
1 tablespoon of cornstarch
2 tablespoons of cold water

$\frac{1}{8}$ teaspoon of almond extract
2 cans of biscuits
4 tablespoons of butter
1 cup of sugar
$\frac{1}{2}$ teaspoon of cinnamon
$\frac{1}{8}$ teaspoon of cloves
$\frac{1}{8}$ teaspoon of nutmeg

Cooking Tools

measuring cups
large saucepan
wooden spoon
measuring spoons
8-inch baking dish
knife

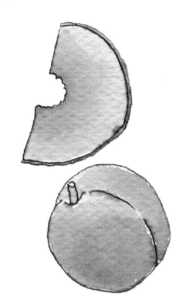

Directions

1. Preheat oven to 400 degrees.
2. Put peaches in saucepan, and add 1 $\frac{1}{2}$ cups water and 1 $\frac{1}{4}$ cups of sugar; stir well.
3. Bring mixture to a boil.
4. Mix together 1 tablespoon of cornstarch and 2 tablespoons of cold water to make a smooth paste.
5. Pour the cornstarch mixture into the peach mixture, and stir for a few minutes until the peach sauce becomes clear.
6. Add the almond extract, and stir well.
7. Remove pan from heat, and pour the peach mixture into the baking dish.
8. Open the cans of biscuits, and cut each biscuit in half. Place the biscuits on top of the peach mixture, and dot them with butter.

9. Combine sugar, cinnamon, cloves, and nutmeg, and sprinkle over top.
10. Bake for 30 minutes.
11. Serve with heavy cream or ice cream.

Cool-and-Crunchy Parfaits

Makes 4 servings

We often make these delicious parfaits. They're a popular Critter Cotillion dessert. They're good any time of the year, but we especially like them in the summer because there's no cooking, no fuss, and no muss. (Well, not much muss anyway.)

Fixings

14 sandwich cookies
8 ounces of nondairy whipped topping

Cooking Tools

airtight plastic bag
large spoon
4 (6-ounce) dessert glasses

Directions

1. Put cookies in the plastic bag.
2. Slowly press the air out of the bag, and seal it.
3. Press on the bag until the cookies are crushed.
4. Spoon about a $\frac{1}{2}$ inch of cookies into the bottom of each glass.
5. Spoon about a $\frac{1}{2}$ inch layer of whipped topping onto cookie layer.
6. Repeat steps 4 and 5 two more times, making sure the top layer is whipped topping.
7. Refrigerate for 1 hour and serve.

Honeycombs

Makes 30 Honeycombs

Robin Rat isn't the only one with a sweet tooth. We have one too, and when it kicks in we like to make this easy and healthy candy.

Fixings

1 (3.2-ounce) package of powdered milk
¾ cup of peanut butter
½ cup of honey

Cooking Tools

mixing spoon
measuring cups
mixing bowl
waxed paper
platter

Directions

1. Stir powdered milk, peanut butter, and honey in a mixing bowl until the milk is absorbed.
2. Form mixture into balls, and place on waxed paper on a platter.
3. Refrigerate for 30 minutes.

MALCOLM CAT

Malcolm is an ugly, battle-scarred, gray cat. He wandered into the yard one day looking for a home, and the farm looked like a pretty good place.

All the animals welcomed Malcolm except Roscoe, one of the raccoon twins. But they became friends as soon as Roscoe realized that Malcolm was not going to steal his prize cherries.

Happily, Malcolm not only found a home, but he also found a pretty wife. Her name is Callie, and she's as pretty as a calendar girl. She devotes her time to chasing butterflies and picking wildflowers. She doesn't think Malcolm looks ugly or battle-scarred, and you must admit he looks a lot better since he got married.

Malcolm has even learned to cook. His recipes and homemaking ideas delight Callie and the other animals when he brings them to the Critter Cotillion. Here he is to share some of his most special secrets.

Place Mats

 I love the little extra touches that make a meal cozy. For a special evening with my wife, Callie, I make beautiful place mats to dress up the table. I make lots of these to use as gifts for our Christmas Critter Cotillion. Here's how to do it.

Tools

construction paper (one sheet for each place mat needed)
crayons or markers
plastic wrap
tape

Directions

1. Decorate construction paper (glitter, glue, and magazine pictures make pretty decorations for these place mats).
2. Lay the construction paper face down on a sheet of plastic wrap, and neatly fold the plastic wrap around the paper so that the folded parts are in the back. Tape the plastic wrap in place.

Apple Cider

Makes 8-10 8-ounce servings
This will warm the bones of even the coldest cat.

Fixings

$\frac{1}{2}$ gallon of apple juice
2 cups of orange juice
$\frac{1}{2}$ cup of lemon juice
$\frac{1}{2}$ cup of powdered sugar
2 tablespoons of cinnamon

Cooking Tools

Crockpot or other slow cooker
mixing spoon

Directions

1. Turn cooker to "high" setting.
2. Pour apple juice, orange juice, and lemon juice into cooker, and stir.
3. When juices are hot, slowly add powdered sugar, and stir until dissolved.
4. Add cinnamon, and mix well.
5. Let simmer for 20 to 30 minutes, and serve hot.

Malcolm Cat's Tuna-and-Cucumber Sandwiches

Makes 40 small sandwiches
My favorite lunch. This is what Callie and I love to take
on a picnic, too.

Fixings

2 cans of tuna
lemon juice
dash of black pepper
soft butter
1 loaf of thinly sliced white bread
1 fresh cucumber cut into thin slice

Cooking Tools

can opener
mixing bowl
fork (for mashing)
knife
can opener
platter

Directions

1. With a can opener, open the can of tuna. Carefully pour off the liquid.
2. Pour the tuna in the mixing bowl.
3. Add enough lemon juice to make a paste.
4. Add a dash of black pepper.
5. Add a little soft butter so the mixture spreads easily.
6. Spread the mixture on a slice of bread.
7. Arrange slices of cucumbers on top.
8. Cover with another slice of bread.
9. Cut sandwiches into small triangles.

Salad from the Sea

Makes 12 servings
This shrimp-and-cucumber salad is a cat's dream come true!

Fixings
6 cucumbers
salt
pepper
oil
vinegar
3 cups of diced, cooked shrimp
Special Dressing (see recipe below)
shredded lettuce
sliced stuffed olives

Cooking Tools
knife
spoon
measuring cups
platter

Directions
1. Peel the cucumbers, and cut each one in half.
2. Using spoon, gently spoon out cucumber seeds.
3. Cut a thin slice from the bottom of each cucumber half so it will sit level.
4. Rub the inside of each cucumber half with salt, pepper, oil, and vinegar to taste.
5. Mix shrimp with special dressing, and fill the cucumber boat with the mixture.
6. Arrange the filled cucumber boats on a bed of shredded lettuce, and garnish with sliced olives.

Special Dressing:
Fixings

2 cups of mayonnaise
$\frac{1}{2}$ cup of heavy cream, whipped
$\frac{1}{2}$ cup of chili sauce
$\frac{1}{4}$ cup of finely chopped green pepper
$\frac{1}{4}$ cup of finely chopped green onions
dash of salt
dash of pepper
a squirt of lemon juice

Cooking Tools

mixing bowl
mixing spoon

Directions

1. Mix together mayonnaise and whipped heavy cream.
2. Add chili sauce, green pepper, and green onions.
3. Add salt, pepper, and a squirt of lemon juice.

Piled-On Pears

Callie loves these pears, especially with extra cheese on top.

Fixings

1 (8-ounce) can of Bartlett pears
$\frac{1}{2}$ tablespoon of mayonnaise for each pear
$\frac{1}{3}$ cup of grated cheddar cheese
maraschino cherries

Cooking Tools
serving plate
spoon

Directions

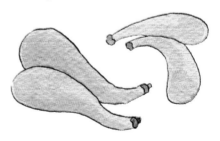

1. Open can of pears, and drain.
2. Place the pears on serving plate.
3. Spoon $\frac{1}{2}$ tablespoon of mayonnaise into the hole in the center of each pear.
4. Sprinkle cheese onto mayonnaise.
5. Top each pear with a cherry.

Squash Casserole

Makes 6 servings

In the summertime while Callie is chasing butterflies and picking wildflowers, I sneak into the garden to pick fresh squash for this recipe.

Fixings
1 egg
1 cup of mayonnaise
1 tablespoon of instant minced onion
$\frac{1}{2}$ teaspoon of garlic powder
$\frac{1}{2}$ teaspoon of salt
$\frac{1}{2}$ teaspoon of pepper
3 cups of fresh squash, sliced and patted dry with paper towels
1 $\frac{1}{2}$ cups of grated sharp cheddar cheese
$\frac{1}{4}$ cup of Parmesan cheese
1 cup of croutons

Cooking Tools
1-quart casserole dish coated with shortening or cooking spray
mixing spoon
paper towels

Directions
1. Preheat oven to 350 degrees.
2. Combine egg, mayonnaise, onion, garlic powder, salt, and pepper in casserole dish.
3. Stir squash and cheeses into egg mixture.
4. Bake for 35 minutes.
5. Top with croutons, and bake an additional 10 minutes.

Busy Biscuits

Makes 14 to 16 biscuits
These biscuits are perfect for a quick breakfast or
afternoon snack.

Fixings

2 $\frac{1}{4}$ cups of baking mix
$\frac{2}{3}$ cup of milk
$\frac{1}{2}$ cup of raisins
$\frac{1}{2}$ tablespoon of cinnamon

Cooking Tools

mixing bowl
mixing spoon
baking sheet covered with aluminum foil

Directions

1. Preheat oven to 450 degrees.
2. Mix all ingredients until a soft dough forms.
3. Drop spoonfuls of mixture onto baking sheet.
4. Bake for 8 to 10 minutes or until golden brown.

My Pies

Makes 20 pies
This recipe is one of my favorites because it's easy and
delicious. Try it for a special dessert at your next celebration.

Fixings

2 cans of biscuits (10 per can)
1 (16-ounce) can of pie filling (cherry, apple, and blueberry are great for
this)

small cup filled with water
melted butter

Cooking Tools
spoon
baking sheet covered with aluminum foil
fork
brush

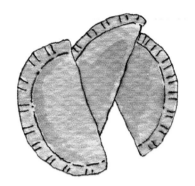

Directions
1. Flatten each biscuit to the size of a pancake.
2. Spoon pie filling onto center of each biscuit, to within 1 inch of the edge. (Don't pile the filling too high or the biscuit won't close over it.)
3. Carefully fold each biscuit into a half-moon shape, and put on the baking sheet.
4. Dip the fork into water, and seal the folded edge of the biscuit, pressing down with the fork going all the way around the folded edge and making "teeth marks" as you go.
5. Brush tops with melted butter.
6. Bake according to biscuit package instructions.

Cranberry Cow
Makes 1 float
Callie and I like to make these on warm afternoons to drink
as we sun ourselves on the back porch of the farmhouse.

Fixings
1 scoop of ice cream
cranberry juice

Cooking Tools
large glass

Directions
1. Scoop ice cream into glass.
2. Slowly pour juice over ice cream.

Chananas
Makes 1 serving
My mom used to make this after-school snack for me. Get
your mom to help you make it, too!

Fixings
1 large banana
2 slices of cheddar cheese

Cooking Tools
knife
toothpick

Directions
1. Cut banana in half
2. Wrap each half in a cheese
3. Secure with a toothpick.

CATHERINE CAT

Whenever you see Catherine Cat, you see her five kittens. Everybody knows that Catherine is looking for a husband. Maybe that's why she's inclined to overdress. She especially likes to wear a large leghorn hat with rows and rows of flowers tied with a huge pink satin bow under her chin. She is criticized by the ladies for her wiggle-waggle walk.

Because she has so many children who eat so much, Catherine always brings an extra dish to Critter Cotillion. At one gathering she brought a special dish for Sam from Siam, whom she hoped to marry. Catherine looked mysterious and triumphant as Sam peered into the tin that she held. "What is it?" he said.

After she told him it was her Secret Golden Raisin Pudding Cake, Sam tried it and loved it so much he ate it all up! But he still didn't marry Catherine. Oh well. She's still looking for an eligible bachelor, but in the meantime she makes fun surprises and tasty treats for her little kittens. Here she is with some of her favorite recipes.

Catherine's Secret Golden Raisin Pudding Cake

Makes 8 servings

This sweet baked pudding is dressed up by the surprising addition of golden raisins. They taste good, too! If you don't have golden raisins, you can use regular ones, or even some nice fresh berries.

Fixings

1 cup of butter
1 cup of sifted flour
1 cup of sugar
1 teaspoon of cinnamon
1 teaspoon of baking soda
1 teaspoon of allspice
$\frac{1}{2}$ teaspoon of nutmeg
3 eggs, well-beaten
1 cup of buttermilk
$\frac{1}{2}$ cup of golden raisins

Cooking Tools

large mixing bowl
medium-sized mixing bowl
egg beater
measuring spoons
measuring cups
2-quart casserole dish coated with shortening or cooking spray

Directions

1. Preheat oven to 400 degrees.
2. Cream butter in the large bowl.
3. Mix together flour, sugar, cinnamon, baking soda, allspice, and nutmeg in the medium-sized bowl.

4. Add the flour mixture to the creamed butter, and mix well. Add the beaten eggs, and buttermilk, and stir well.
5. Add the golden raisins, and stir gently.
6. Pour the mixture into the casserole dish, and bake for about 1 hour or until the pudding is set.

Homemade Fundough

This is not for eating.
The kittens love to play with this, and they often mold it into shapes like my hat or the big bow I wear under my chin.

Fixings

1 cup of flour
1 cup of water
1 teaspoon of baby oil
2 teaspoons of cream of tartar
$\frac{1}{2}$ cup of salt
food coloring

Cooking Tools

saucepan
airtight container

Directions

1. Mix all of the ingredients in the saucepan.
2. Cook over low heat, stirring constantly, until the mixture loosens from the sides of the pan and forms a ball.
3. Allow fundough to cool, and store it in the airtight container.

Macaroni Necklace

This is not for eating.
I like to wear a homemade necklace to special gatherings of the
animals—just in case there might be a nice gentleman there.

Tools

elbow macaroni
yarn

Directions

1. String the macaroni onto the yarn in a beautiful pattern.
2. Tie the necklace around your neck.

Catherine's Kitten Rollers

Makes 4 sandwiches
I make these round sandwiches for picnics and to put in the
kittens' lunch bags for something good to eat at school.

Fixings

1 (5-ounce) can of chopped ham
$\frac{1}{3}$ cup of low-fat mayonnaise
1 tablespoon of butter
1 tablespoon of mustard
$\frac{1}{2}$ tablespoon of poppy seeds
4 hamburger buns
4 slices of Swiss cheese

Cooking Tools

small mixing bowl
mixing spoon
knife for spreading
baking sheet covered with aluminum foil

Directions

1. Preheat oven to 325 degrees.
2. Mix ham, mayonnaise, butter, and mustard in the mixing bowl.
3. Stir in the poppy seeds.
4. Spread the mixture onto the bottom of each hamburger bun.
5. Top with one slice of cheese and top of the bun.
6. Place sandwiches on baking sheet, and bake 10 to 15 minutes or until the cheese melts.

Pint-sized Pizzas

Makes 12 pizzas
The kittens meow with approval when I let them make these fun, yummy pizzas.

Fixings

6 English muffins, split in half
1 jar of spaghetti sauce
pepperoni slices
mushroom slices
Parmesan cheese
any other pizza topping

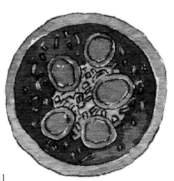

Cooking Tools

spoon
baking sheet covered with aluminum foil

Directions

1. Preheat oven to 350 degrees.
2. Place English muffin halves on baking sheet.
3. Spoon spaghetti sauce onto muffins, spreading evenly.
4. Layer pepperoni, mushrooms, and cheese or other toppings onto sauce.
5. Bake 5 to 10 minutes or until warm and crispy.

Spicy Taters

Makes 4 servings
Spicy Taters are an easy dish to take to Critter Cotillion, and
the ducks especially love their zesty taste.

Fixings

1 (12-ounce) can of small white potatoes
water
1 tablespoon of paprika

Cooking Tools

small saucepan
spoon

Directions

1. Open the can of potatoes, and drain them.
2. Pour the potatoes into the saucepan, and add ⅔ can of water.
3. Sprinkle paprika onto potatoes.
4. Simmer, stirring occasionally, for 10 to 15 minutes or until the potatoes
   are warm and most of the water has evaporated.

Critter Cakes

Makes 10 cakes
This is the all-time favorite of the critters on the farm.

Fixings

1 can of biscuits
orange marmalade
raisins
cinnamon
vanilla icing

Cooking Tools

spoon
baking sheet covered with aluminum foil

Directions

1. Preheat oven according to biscuit package directions.
2. Place biscuits on baking sheet, and flatten each biscuit to the size of a pancake.
3. Spread a small spoonful of marmalade onto each biscuit.
4. Sprinkle raisins and cinnamon onto marmalade.
5. Bake according to package directions.
6. Spread on the vanilla icing before the biscuits cool.

Sugar Sweet Mice

Makes 8-10 mice

These candy mice are the kittens' delight. I always make them on special occasions, especially at Christmas.

Fixings

6 cups of powdered sugar
3 tablespoons of light corn syrup
1 egg white
$\frac{1}{8}$ teaspoon of pure vanilla
pink food coloring
a piece of white string about 2 inches long
silver or gold candy balls

Cooking Tools

measuring cups   small saucepan
measuring spoons   fork
sifter
mixing bowl

Directions

1. Sift powdered sugar into the mixing bowl.
2. Warm the corn syrup in the small saucepan until it is really smooth, and then use a fork to stir in the powdered sugar and egg white.
3. Add the vanilla, and knead with your hands until the mixture is smooth like velvet (have your adult helper show you how to knead).
4. Divide the mixture into 3 or 4 pieces. Leave some white, and tint some pale pink, making sure the food coloring is evenly distributed.
5. Dust a space on the table and also dust your hands with powdered sugar; and then shape the mixture into small "mice" about 2 inches long.

To make the mice: Mold a small "sausage" shape, pointing it at the nose end (which is kind of sharp). Tie a knot in the end of the string, and press the knot under the mouse where the tail should be.

To make the ears: Make two tiny balls from the pink dough. Flatten them, and use your thumb to press out a curve. Place them where the ears should be on the mouse's head.

To make the eyes: Press silver or gold candy balls into place on the mouse's face. Let mouse dry.

Whisker Sticks

Whenever I make a pie, I give the leftover crust to the kittens to make this tasty treat. It's so easy!

Fixings

leftover pie crust scraps
butter
cinnamon
sugar

Cooking Tools

knife
baking sheet covered with aluminum foil

Directions

1. Preheat oven to 325 degrees.
2. Cut pie crust into small strips, and place them on the baking sheet.
3. Sprinkle with cinnamon and sugar.
4. Bake about 5 to 10 minutes until golden brown and crispy.

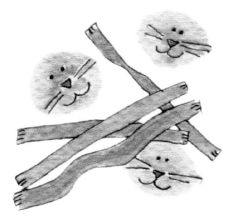

EMERALD RIVER CRITTER COTILLION

"What fun we'll have tonight!" That's what every animal is thinking when we start getting ready for our monthly shindig.

Red-Rip and Cleopatra supervise the picking of the vegetables. Mr. Frog prepares a speech. And of course, he is in charge of the tea. Robin Rat leads recreation, which is usually highlighted by a bubble-blowing contest.

Que and Quan decorate the trees with nutter cones, while Roscoe and Sweet William tune up their fiddles. Malcolm cooks up such a storm there is steam billowing from his kitchen. And Catherine brings lots and lots of Critter Cakes.

Neighboring animals from all along the banks of Emerald River also come to our gathering. A flock of fireflies who call themselves the "Nightlight Battalion" hover over the whole area, lighting up the good food and smiling faces.

The peacocks always get attention by spreading their beautiful feathers. Malachi the Mole, who is shamelessly lazy and always late, forgets to bring a dish but makes it just in time for the festivities every month.

Cyrus Cricket is a pleasant fellow who is always welcome because he provides music for the dancing by rubbing his back legs together to make beautiful sounds. He also plays the mouth harp. He drives a tricycle and pops wheelies to show off to the ladies and disturb the fellows.

Mr. Frog, of course, disapproves of Cyrus's shenanigans with the tricycles, but he dances to the cricket's music until his legs turn to jelly.

Hilda, the huge Great Dane, always comes. Some of the animals call her the "Biscuit Hound" because she eats a lot. Sometimes she scares us because of her size. She does a great job protecting all of us, though, and so deserves to eat all she wants.

A few of the beavers usually show up, but they eat in a hurry and can't stay long because upkeep on their dams in the river is time-consuming work.

Jeweled dragonflies hover about, perching on the tips of the tree limbs and then darting swiftly away carrying their favorite bread.

The otter that lives in the rushes by the river stops by to eat and swim in the duck pond. He shows off his barrel roll tricks and jumps in and out of the water to entertain the younger animals. His sleek furry head and soft round eyes always appear at the table early because he works up such an appetite.

Always last to appear is a rickety buggy drawn by a fat swayback horse named Sassafras and driven by a reckless black cat named Klondike. All the animals who want a ride to our gathering stand by the road and wait for Klondike and Sassafras to come by and pick them up.

Once all the animals arrive, it's time to eat! Here are a few of our favorite Critter Cotillion menus that you and your friends might like to try. They're perfect for tea parties and other gatherings.